Baby Day

by Susan Heyboer O'Keefe
Illustrated by Robin Spowart

Boyds Mills Press

Text copyright © 2006 by Susan Heyboer O'Keefe
Illustrations copyright © 2006 by Robin Spowart

Published by Boyds Mills Press, Inc.
A Highlights Company
815 Church Street
Honesdale, Pennsylvania 18431
Printed in China

Library of Congress Cataloging-in-Publication Data (U.S.)

O'Keefe, Susan Heyboer.
Baby day / by Susan Heyboer O'Keefe ; illustrated by Robin Spowart.
— 1st ed.
p. cm.
Summary: In rhyming text, babies are described participating in
activities, from laughing and crying to playing Pat-a-cake and Peek-a-boo.
ISBN 1-56397-981-0 (alk. paper)
[1. Babies—Fiction. 2. Stories in rhyme.]   I. Spowart, Robin, ill.
II. Title.
PZ8.3.O37Bab 2006
[E]—dc22   2005020114

First edition, 2006
The text of this book is set in 24-point Optima.
The illustrations are done in pastel.

Visit our Web site at www.boydsmillspress.com

10 9 8 7 6 5 4 3 2 1

For Michaela
—S. H. O.

To Bing Thomas, loving friend to children everywhere
—R. S.

Baby high

Baby low

Baby fast

Baby slow

Baby laugh

Baby cry

Baby wet

Baby dry

Baby work is never done.
Good thing baby work is fun.

Peek-a-boo

Whirly-go

Pat-a-cake

Bubble blow

Upsy-daisy

Coo-chee-coo

Piggy count

Kissy poo

Baby play makes every day
a giggly goofy holiday.

Darkened sky

Starry wink

Baby yawn

Baby blink

Baby book

Baby bear

Cozy quilt

Rocking chair

Baby sleep is sweet as pie,
head on shoulder, hush-a-bye